For Milo,
our very own Space cadet

First published in 2009 in Great Britain by
Gullane Children's Books
185 Fleet Street London EC4A 2HS
www.gullanebooks.com

1 3 5 7 9 10 8 6 4 2

Text and illustrations © Diane & Christyan Fox 2009

The right of Diane & Christyan Fox to be identified as the author and illustrator of this work
has been asserted by them in accordance with the Copyright, Designs and Patents Act, 1988.
A CIP record for this title is available from the British Library.

HB ISBN: 978-1-86233-712-1
pb ISBN: 978-1-86233-774-9

Printed and bound in Indonesia

Little Tom
and the Trip to the Moon

Diane and Christyan Fox

GULLANE
CHILDREN'S BOOKS

What are you painting, Little Tom?

It's not a painting.
These are my . . .
plans!

Why are you wearing
Wellington boots, Little Tom?

They're not Wellingtons,
they're . . .

...anti-gravity boots!

Why have you got those bottles, Little Tom?

They're not bottles, they're . . .

What's the cardboard box for, Little Tom?

It's not a box, it's a...

...helmet!

Another helmet, Little Tom?

It's not a helmet, it's a...

So that's where my kitchen things went, Little Tom?

They're not kitchen things, they're...

...flight controls!
3-2-1
BLAST OFF!

It's bathtime, Little Tom.
Are you still playing?

I'm not playing, I'm...

So, is this bath a
moon pool, Little Tom?

Don't be silly.
It's not a bath.
It's my...

...PIRATE SHIP!

Other Gullane Children's Books for you to enjoy.

My Dad
Charles Fuge

Imagine Me A Pirate!
Mark Marshall

Ferdie and the Falling Leaves
Julia Rawlinson

Illustrated by
Tiphanie Beeke

Holly's Red Boots
Francesca Chessa